MARTHA OSPINA

Pergamano®

'TH… FUN'

LRV Kreatief

★ Pergamano is the trade name under which the designs and materials for the parchment craft is put on the market.

Second Edition

Cover: Erik Uitenbogaard
Photography: Studio Ton Kruithof, Kampen
Typesetting: Stand By, Nieuwegein
Translation: E. van Westendorp, Bilthoven
Printing: Van der Weij BV Grafische Bedrijven, Hilversum

ISBN 90 384 0968 0
NUGI 440

CONTENTS

1. INTRODUCTION

When I wrote my first book '*Pergamano, cards made from parchment paper*' – in 1989 – I could not have imagined that Parchment Craft would be picked up so quickly by the Dutch and Belgian hobbyists. After all, the new craft was totally unknown. Normally it takes quite a while before a new hobby becomes widely known, but with Parchment Craft it all happened very quickly. The publisher definitely noticed this from the number of Pergamano books that were sold in the first year.

Basic techniques

In my first book I only described the materials and tools and explained the basic techniques of the hobby. The pieces of work that were described were single cards and folded cards. The first Pergamano book was made for those people who had not yet heard of the craft. Because of the success of my first book '*Pergamano, cards made from parchment paper*', the publisher asked me to write a second book on the same subject, but with more possibilities. I indeed had more creative ideas for working with parchment paper, which resulted in the book: '*New ideas with Pergamano*'.

Three-dimensional techniques

In that second book I gave further information about the basic techniques, gave some hints and explained the new 3-D technique. 3-D stands for three-dimensional technique. It means that when making the pieces of work, we do not just work on the ordinary flat surface but we raise some parts of the piece. For instance, we trace a flower from a pattern a second time on a separate piece of parchment paper, paint, emboss, perforate and cut out, and then we glue this part 'raised' onto the same flower on the card. The 'raised' glueing is done with a thick sticky glue called PERGAKIT. Cards with one or more 3-D elements are very beautiful, especially when we see shadow effects due to the incidence of light.

Three-dimensional objects

The 3-D technique is an important addition to the basic techniques of Parchment Craft. With this technique we have made the first step towards three-dimensional objects like boxes and dolls.

Boxes

This book shows you not only how to make boxes of all shapes and sizes, but also how to make a cradle, an angel, a basket and a mobile.

When the publisher asked me to write a book on boxes, I doubted whether I had enough ideas and patterns to make an interesting book, but when I talked about the idea for this book to Corrie Daniels (one of my students), my doubts disappeared quickly. Corrie appeared to be a 'boxes freak': she had already made many of them in various shapes and sizes. They all looked beautiful.

Together we selected the designs, made the patterns and, not forgetting, made the pieces of work for the pictures. We enjoyed working together and complemented each other well as far as creative ideas and workmanship were concerned.
Corrie, I would like to thank you again for your help.

This book is about boxes and other three-dimensional objects, all made from parchment paper and worked with the parchment techniques. I hope that with this book I have added an extra dimension to the Parchment Craft hobby.

I am always open to constructive criticism on the contents of this book, so please send any comments, suggestions or remarks to the publisher.

Pergamano
"Kaarten maken van perkamentpapier"
pergakit
voor/für/for/pour
PINTURA
TINTA
Puntschaartje Edelstaal
Spitzschere Edelstahl
pointus en métal précieux
pointed scissors

2. MATERIALS AND TOOLS

2.1 Basic materials and tools

What do you need to make the boxes and other 3-D objects shown in this book? First of all you will need materials and tools that were developed especially for working with parchment paper, including the parchment paper itself. They are listed below:

Parchment paper
Pergamano parchment paper (weight 150 gr/m^2), available in blocks of 25 sheets size A4 (210 x 297 mm), and in blocks of 12 sheets size A3 (297 x 420 mm). Blocks size A3 are also available in the quality 'extra strong'.

For tracing and painting with ink:

Tinta
Pergamano Tinta indelible inks in the colours: red, yellow, blue, green, leafgreen, sepia, white, black, turquoise, silver and gold.

Pen
An old type of steel-nibbed mapping pen, e.g. Conté.

For painting:

Pergamano Pintura
Pintura paint in the colours: red (no. 03), yellow (no. 16), blue (no. 02), green (no. 08), light green (no. 04), brown (no. 12), white (no. 01), skin colour (no. 13), purple (no. 07), fuchsia (no. 20), bordeaux (no. 51), cinnamon (no. 52) and black (no. 11).

Brushes
Sable-hair brushes no. 0 and no. 2.

For evenly colouring the reverse side of the parchment paper:

Dorso pastels
Pergamano Dorso pastels in a box with 8 assorted colours: pink, yellow, yellow ocre, blue, green, skin colour, purple and turquoise.

For perforating:

Pergamano single-needle perforating tool
Pergamano two-needle perforating tool
Pergamano 4-needle perforating tool
Pergamano perforating/embossing pad

For embossing:
Pergamano stylus
Pergamano small ball embossing tool
Pergamano large ball embossing tool
Pergamano embossing pad

For cutting:
Pergamano pointed scissors, available in two qualities.

A cutting mat of at least 22 x 29 cms.
A hobby knife
A steel ruler of at least 30 cms.

For glueing
A colourless paper glue (suitable for paper), Pergakit (a transparent viscous kit), double-sided adhesive tape on a holder.

In addition:
A cotton rag to spread out the Dorso pastels, synthetic ribbons in various colours and widths, adhesive tape.

2.2 Properties and applications

Most materials and tools require a bit more information about their properties and applications.
First of all the *parchment paper*:

'extra strong'

For greeting cards we always use parchment paper of 150 gr/m^2. When making three-dimensional objects like boxes, in which the paper should give the piece of work some rigidity, it is necessary you use a thicker type of parchment paper: the quality 'extra strong'. It goes without saying that bigger pieces of work require this stronger quality of paper more than smaller ones.

Greeting cards usually end up in a photo album, safely behind a transparent sheet. They are not often opened and closed, which in the end would weaken the folding line. It is probably that boxes would be picked up, opened and closed more often, which is why you need the stronger quality of paper. It is available in the hobby shops in pads of 12 sheets size A3.

Tinta inks

shake well

Before using the inks, shake them well, especially the colours white, silver and gold.
Gold is the most difficult colour to work with; follow these instructions carefully: shake the bottle well and then stir it with a cocktail stick. Transfer a drop of ink onto the mapping pen by lightly touching the steel nib with the cocktail stick. Repeat this procedure every time you need new ink. This way you will not have any problems with the gold ink!

Pintura paints

diluting

Pintura paints are easy to use as they can be diluted with water, if in case they have dried out a bit. You can dilute the Pintura paint on a saucer: by mixing a drop of paint with a brush that has been dipped into water.

Pintura paints give a glossy effect and dry quickly.

Dorso pastels

rubbing

Dorso is spread easily and evenly by rubbing with a cotton rag or a tissue. Make sure the Dorso is at room temperature when using them.

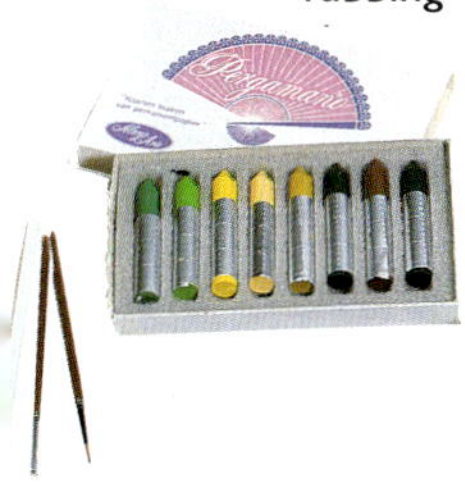

Brushes

Sable-hair brushes are also mentioned in the list of required materials. Of course also synthetic brushes of good quality are available. The price and your personal preference play an important part when you choose.

Perforating tools

In the beginning there were only the 1 and 4 needle tool. Later a 2 and 3 needle tool have been added to the serie.

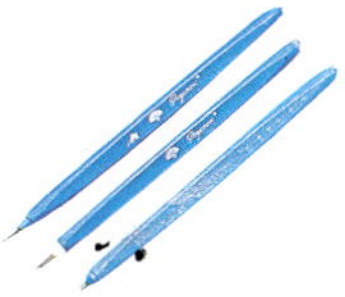

Perforating/embossing pad and embossing pad

For perforating and embossing a felt perforating/embossing pad could do. The special embossing pad however has a big advantage: you can hardly tear the paper, even if you emboss with (too) much pressure. This is because the embossing pad has a hard bottom with a thin, soft top surface; the hard bottom gives adequate support to the parchment paper.

Hard bottom

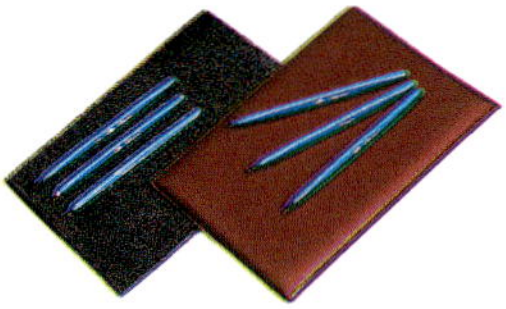

Pointed scissors

Two qualities of pointed scissors are available. One quality has bigger handles and is therefore more suitable for people with thicker fingers.

Cutting mat

A cutting mat is very easy to use, but not strictly necessary. A piece of cardboard of at least 2 mm can also be of service when cutting the parchment paper.

a sheet of cardboard

Hobby knife

These knifes are available everywhere and are not expensive. They are very sharp, so be careful! After some time the cutting edge of the blade will become a bit dull. Break off one segment of the blade and your knife is as good as new again.

Steel ruler

The only suitable ruler is a steel ruler or a ruler made from different material but with a steel edge to cut along. Rulers made from aluminium or other materials are too soft. The hobby knife tends to cut into such ruler a bit and then the knife gets stuck.

steel edge

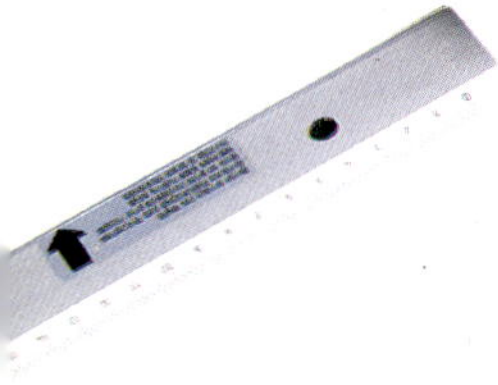

Adhesives

Glueing can be done in several ways:

a. with colourless paper glue or white glue that dries up colourless
b. with Pergakit, a thick glue that sticks well to parchment paper and that does not have to pre-dry.
c. with double-sided adhesive tape (colourless).
d. ordinary mat white or colourless adhesive tape.

holder Always buy adhesive tape in a holder. You really need it and it prevents a lot of irritation.

Ribbons (cotton or synthetic ribbons)

splicing Ribbons are available in a great variety of colours and widths. Ribbons with a width of less than 4 mm are however not easy to find. That's why we make them ourselves. Choose a synthetic ribbon in the colour of your choice and perforate it with the single-needle perforating tool at a 2 mm distance from the side. Now pull the ribbon in such a way that the needle splices the ribbon in two parts. This way you can splice synthetic ribbons into two narrower parts.

3. TECHNIQUES

3.1 Current techniques

The techniques we use to make the three-dimensional objects are the same as the techniques we use to make greeting cards. We assume that these techniques are known, they have been explained extensively (with the help of pictures) in the book 'Pergamano, cards made from parchment paper' by Martha Ospina (book number ISBN 90 3840 3437 from the publishers: La Rivière & Voorhoeve, Kampen, The Netherlands).

These techniques are:

tracing Tracing with Tinta
dorsing Dorsing with Dorso pastels
painting Painting with Tinta and Pintura
perforating Perforating with the perforating tools
embossing Embossing with the embossing tools
cutting Cutting with the Pergamano pointed scissors.

The new techniques are: folding and glueing.

3.2 Folding

right angles

When we made folded greeting cards we learned to flatten the fold by lightly rubbing over it with the index finger; the fold should not be made too sharp in order to avoid the paper from cracking. When making boxes, this also applies, of course. Contrary to greeting cards, three-dimensional objects are usually folded in right angles. We fold the paper a bit further than up to the right angle; after 'springing back' it will assume more or less the proper right angle.

scoring
embossing pad

To facilitate the folding we first score the parchment paper on the folding line. Scoring is a technical term from the cardboard industry. Cardboard is scored where it has to be folded. With Pergamano the scoring is called embossing, and it is done with the small ball embossing tool. We advise you to use the embossing pad underneath your paper while you emboss.
In the patterns for the boxes we use ordinary lines and dashed lines; dashed lines indicate folding lines. All dashed lines have to be embossed.

reverse side When we described the basic techniques in the book *'Pergamano, cards made from parchment paper'*, we learned that embossing is usually done on the reverse side of the piece of work. When we have to emboss on the front side it is indicated in the pattern. The same rules apply for making boxes: we emboss folding lines on the reverse side. If we have to emboss on the front side, it is indicated with the letters '**cv**'.

embossing folding lines When do we emboss folding lines on the front side and when on the reverse side? We emboss folding lines on the side that becomes inside after folding, because the parchment paper is then easier folded in that direction. Now you understand that when making boxes the embossing of the folding lines is usually done on the reverse side: the rest of the work has been done on the outside of the box.

ruler Always emboss folding lines with the help of a ruler because they have to be straight.

3.3 Making glued joints

good glue The glueing of the joints of three-dimensional objects can sometimes be difficult. The following hints might help. Firstly, you need good glue. Secondly, follow the glueing instructions the manufacturer put on the wrapping of the glue. And then:

stress-free Fold your piece of work in such a way that it already has the shape it eventually should get (make it stress-free).

pre-dry Apply a thin layer of glue on the glueing strip and let it pre-dry if so indicated in the glueing instructions. Glue the parts that have to be glued and hold them together with adhesive tape or a paper clip.

one glued joint at a time Only glue one joint at a time if this is possible, depending on the construction of your piece of work,. Let it dry properly before glueing the next joint.

double-sided adhesive tape Another way of making the glued joints is by using double-sided adhesive tape. This method has the advantage that you do not have to wait for the glue to dry and you do not see any smudges through the parchment paper, which may occur when using glue.

disadvantage

A disadvantage is that the glued joint is not very strong and in the end will get loose.
Work this way:
Fold the piece of work into the stress-free shape. Cut off a piece of transparent double-sided adhesive tape of the same length as the glueing strip of your piece of work. Place it onto the glueing strip and bring the joint together. Press well. Sometimes this is not possible because some parts of the three-dimensional objects can not be reached any more from the inside after you have stuck them.

clean and grease-free

When using glues and adhesives the parts that have to be glued must be clean and grease-free. This means that you must not use the greasy Dorso pastels on spots that have to be glued, like the glueing strips. If you accidentally dorsed the glueing strips, you can clean them with a bit of dissolving fluid. The part of the piece of work you are glueing onto should of course also be clean and grease-free. You can add a bit of Dorso on the outside later on.

4. LAY-OUTS (CUT-OUTS)

jagged shape

A lay-out of a three-dimensional object is the shape we get when we unfold the material (the parchment paper in this case) into a flat surface. When, for instance, we want to have the lay-out of an existing box, we open the box, and cut loose the sides somewhere in order to be able to totally unfold the box. Lay-outs usually have a jagged shape.
In this book you will find two inserts on which you will find the lay-outs that are too big to be printed on the pages of the booklet. The lay-outs have been numbered according to the numbers of the pieces of work and the working instructions.

full-scale

The lay-outs have been drawn full-scale. We can trace them as they are and we will get a piece of work of the size as shown on the photograph.

photo-copier

If we want to make the pieces of work a bit bigger or smaller, we can do this by enlarging or reducing the lay-out through photocopying. For enlarging there is one restriction though: the lay-out will still have to fit onto a sheet of Pergamano paper size A3, the largest size available. If we want to enlarge or reduce a box, we can do that the following way. We copy the lay-out of the box on a continuously adjustable photocopier. (You usually find such machines in a photocopy shop). If, for instance, we want to reduce a box by 1/10th, we preset the photocopier to 90%. To enlarge a box by 1/10th, we preset the photocopier to 110%, and if we want to make the box half the size bigger, preset to 150%.
When you enlarge, do pay attention to the fact that the enlarged lay-out should still fit onto a sheet of parchment paper size A3 (297 x 420 mm). You can of course find this out by using the 'try out'-method, but you could also try to calculate it.
For example:
Biggest measurement of the lay-out: 228 mm.
Length of the paper: 420 mm.

The maximum enlargement possible is:

Make these calculations for both directions of the lay-out (in the length and the width of the lay-out and of the sheet of parchment paper).

$$\frac{420}{228} \times 100\% = 130\%$$

For example:
– maximum length of the lay-out: 350 mm
– maximum width of the lay-out: 228 mm
– length sheet size A3: 420 mm
– width sheet size A3: 297 mm.

The maximum enlargement in the length will be:

$$\frac{420}{350} \times 100\% = 120\%$$

The maximum enlargement in the width will be:

$$\frac{297}{228} = 130\%$$

Choose the enlargement at 120% (which is the smallest percentage).

adapt perforation pattern

N.B.: When you enlarge or reduce, the perforation pattern will also change size and you will not be able to perforate exactly on the indicated four little dots with the 4-needle perforating tool. When you enlarge to more than 130% or reduce to less than 90% this will give you problems in perforating and cutting. You will then have to adapt the perforation pattern yourself.

5. GENERAL INSTRUCTIONS

In this chapter we explain step by step how to make three-dimensional objects like boxes. They are general instructions, that usually apply to most of the pieces of work. Specific instructions *per piece of work* will follow after this chapter

The working environment

It is probably unnecessary, but before we begin I would like to say something about your working environment.
The general area should be uncluttered; you will need a table which should be flat, a good chair and a cutting board or a piece of cardboard. Most importantly you will need good light, positioned in such a way that your hands do not overshadow your work.

Think twice before you begin

Always first examine the pattern (the lay-out) and the picture of the piece of work closely, and carefully read the instructions before you start to work.

Fixing the parchment paper

adhesive tape

Take a sheet of parchment paper that is big enough for the lay-out, and tape it onto the pattern with two pieces of adhesive tape.

Tracing

photocopy

Trace the whole lay-out (except for the perforation pattern) with a white pencil or white Tinta ink. When perforating, we perforate the parchment paper and the pattern together. If you do not want to damage the pattern, you will have to make a photocopy of it first.

Dorsing

basic techniques

When you have to dorse, follow the instructions given in the basic instructions. Dorse where indicated and in the colours mentioned in the working instructions.

Painting

Follow the instructions given when painting with Pintura or Tinta.

Perforating

4-needle tool

Perforate with the 4-needle perforating tool as indicated in the perforation patterns.

Embossing

repeated figures

Emboss as instructed. In the patterns you will usually find repeated figures, e.g. flower figures of which some have been indicated in black. This indicates that *all* similar figures have to be embossed. Dashed lines (= folding lines) always have to be embossed with the help of a ruler. When dashed lines have been marked 'c.v.', it means that they have to be embossed on the *front side*. If the lines have not been marked, it means they have to be embossed on the reverse side.

Perforating and cutting

Cut out straight lines with the help of a hobby knife and a ruler. Cut out curved lines with the Pergamano pointed scissors. If you see small dots along the curved lines, perforate the small dots with the single-needle or the two-needle perforating tool. There are two ways of perforating with the two-needle perforating tool: you insert one needle in the previous hole (so you just add one hole) in order to secure an even distance between the holes or you add two new holes every time you perforate, which method of course is twice as fast. After perforating, carefully take off superfluous paper.

Cutting the perforations

Cut the 4-hole perforations into cross-shaped holes or slits with the Pergamano pointed scissors.

Folding

embossed folding lines

Fold the parchment paper as indicated by the embossed folding lines. Fold the parchment paper almost double, and then back to the angle it should get (usually this is a right angle = a 90° angle) If you do this properly, the parchment paper will stay in the angle you want.

Glueing

transparent glue

Try to fold the whole piece of work into its final shape by re-adjusting the folds if necessary. The glueing is a lot easier if the non-glued piece of work already has its final shape. Put a bit of transparent glue onto one of the glueing strips. Follow the instructions given by the manufacturer of the glue as far as amount of layers, drying time etc. is concerned. You can keep the glued joints together with adhesive tape or a paper clip.
First let the glued joint dry properly before you start glueing a second one.
Note: all pieces of work are different, so carefully follow the instructions given with each individual piece of work in this book.

FLAT BOX

General
This is a simple box that does not require any glueing.

Tracing
Trace with a white pencil: contours and the folding lines.
Tinta white: all scalloped lines.
Tinta gold: trace a second scalloped line just outside the white scalloped lines; the scalloped lines around the perforation patterns.

Perforating
As in perforation patterns.

Embossing
The figures indicated in black, all scalloped lines, the folding lines.

Cutting
Cut the 4-hole perforations into cross-shaped holes and slits.

Perforating and cutting out
Cut out the lay-out, cut in the line x-x. Perforate and cut out as indicated by the dotted lines.

Folding
Fold the lay-out into a box and insert the V-shaped overlap into the incision x-x.

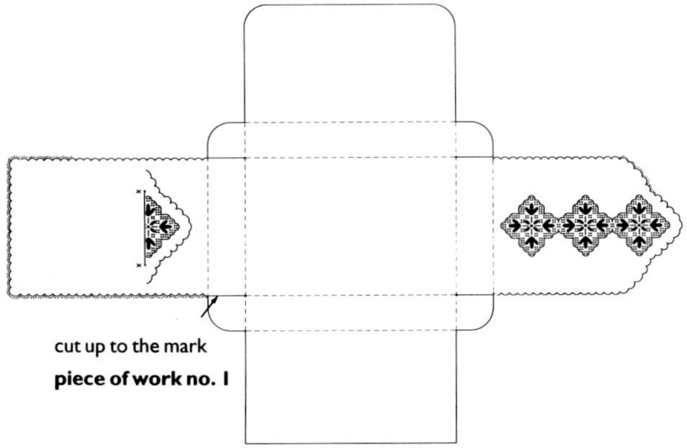

PYRAMID

Tracing
Tinta sepia: the bricks and face; Tinta black: the nose, eyes, mouth, eyebrows, eyelashes and collar; Tinta white: the folding lines and the glueing strips of the pyramid.

Dorsing
Dorso yellow ocre: evenly dorse the whole surface of the lay-out (except for the glueing strips), on the front side and on the reverse side of the parchment paper.
N.B.: dorse the face only on the reverse side.

Painting
Tinta gold and black: use a brush to paint the stripes around the face alternately in gold and black.

Embossing
On the front side, with the small ball embossing tool: the sepia contours of the bricks. Emboss little stripes at both ends of each brick.
On the reverse side: all folding lines.

Cutting out
Cut out the lay-out along the contours.

Folding
Fold the pyramid in a triangular shape and glue all glueing strips in one go. Keep the glued joints together with adhesive tape till the glue has dried. Take off the adhesive tape.

piece of work no. 2

BUTTERFLY BOX

General
The butterfly serves as a fastener for the two lids. The wings are bent upwards and slipped through opening 'A'. The butterfly is strengthened with an extra glued-on butterfly 'B', that has been painted.

Extra materials required
2 pieces of gold thread for the feelers.

Tracing
With a white pencil: all contours and folding lines, except the two butterflies; Tinta white: the butterfly on the lid; Tinta black: butterfly 'B'.

Dorsing
Dorso yellow ocre: the whole lay-out, except for the glueing strip.

Painting
Paint butterfly 'B' in three colours: Pintura orange (red + yellow): the parts marked 'or'; Pintura yellow: the parts marked 'ge'; Tinta black: the parts marked 'T.zw'. The body of the butterfly: alternately Tinta black and Pintura yellow.

Perforating
As in perforation patterns.

Embossing
The black figures in the perforation patterns, the black parts of butterfly 'B', the folding lines, the scalloped lines on the lids.

Cutting
Cut the 4-hole perforations into cross-shaped holes and slits. Cut the connections between the perforations along the contours of the lids and take off superfluous paper.

Perforating and cutting out
Cut out the lay-out (also opening 'A'). Perforate and cut out as indicated by the dotted lines.
N.B.: the butterfly on the lid remains attached only in the middle.

Glueing

Glue the painted butterfly 'B' onto the butterfly on the lid with a thin layer of Pergakit and insert the two feelers in between the two layers of parchment paper.

Folding and glueing

Fold the box and glue the vertical glueing strip; close the bottom, first fold part 1, than 2, 3 and 4.

Finishing off

Bend the wings of the butterfly together and slip them through opening 'A'.

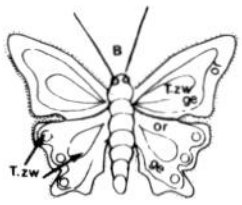

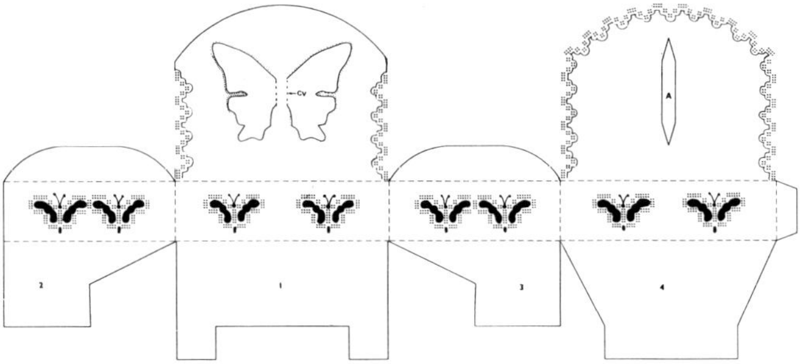

piece of work no. 3

SQUARE BOX

General
This is a square box that has two interlocking lids, one on the top and one on the bottom.

Tracing
With a white pencil: the contours and folding lines;
Tinta white: the scalloped lines.

Dorsing
Dorso blue: the surfaces marked 'D.bl'; Dorso pink: the surfaces marked 'D.rs'.

Perforating
As in perforation patterns.

Embossing
The decorations marked in black; the scalloped lines, the vertical lines in the diamonds; the folding lines (also the oblique folding lines).

Cutting
Cut the 4-hole perforations into cross-shaped holes and slits.

Perforating and cutting out
Cut out the lay-out; perforate and cut out as indicated by the dotted lines.

Folding and glueing
Fold the box and glue the two glueing strips.

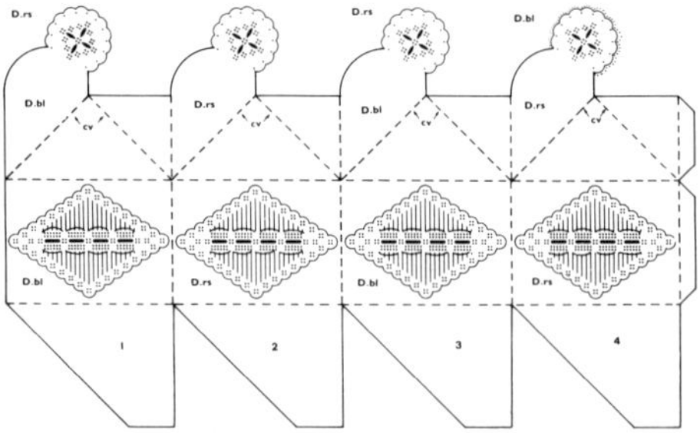

piece of work no. 4

LITTLE HAND BAG

General
This is a simple box that does not require any glueing.

Tracing
With a white pencil: the contours and folding lines; Tinta white: the scalloped lines.

Dorsing
Dorso blue: the whole lay-out.

Painting
Paint the crosses indicated in black with Pintura blue.

Perforating
As in perforation patterns.

Embossing
The blue crosses, the scalloped lines, the folding lines.

Cutting
Cut the 4-hole perforations into cross-shaped holes and slits. Cut loose flap 'A' on three sides only, totally cut out opening 'B'.

Perforating and cutting out
Cut out the lay-out; Cut in the line x-x; perforate and cut out as indicated by the dotted lines.

Folding and glueing
Fold the box and insert flap 'A' into the incision x-x.

PAINTED BOX

Tracing
With a white pencil: the contours and folding lines; Tinta white: the petals, the decorative lines, the scalloped lines; Tinta sepia: the leaves.

Painting

Pintura purple + white (make colour differentiations): the petals ; Pintura green + Tinta sepia: the leaves; Pintura orange (red + yellow): the flower hearts.

Perforating

As in perforation patterns.

Embossing

The petals, all dots, the decorative lines, the scalloped lines, the folding lines.

Cutting

Cut the 4-hole perforations into cross-shaped holes and slits.

Perforating and cutting out

Cut out the lay-out; perforate and cut out as indicated by the dotted lines.

Folding and glueing

Fold the box and glue the two glueing strips. Interlock the parts of the lid (see picture).

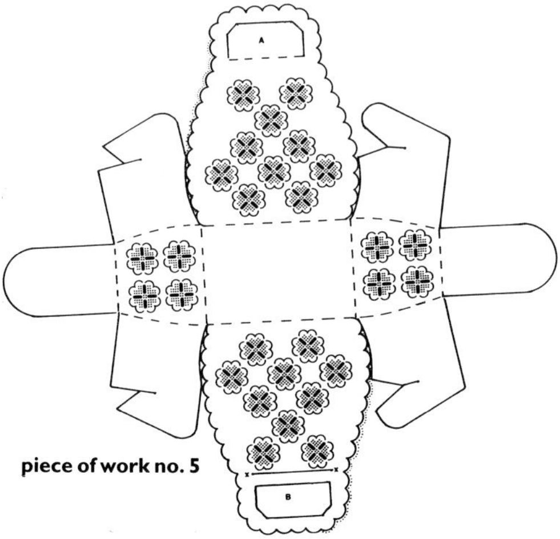

piece of work no. 5

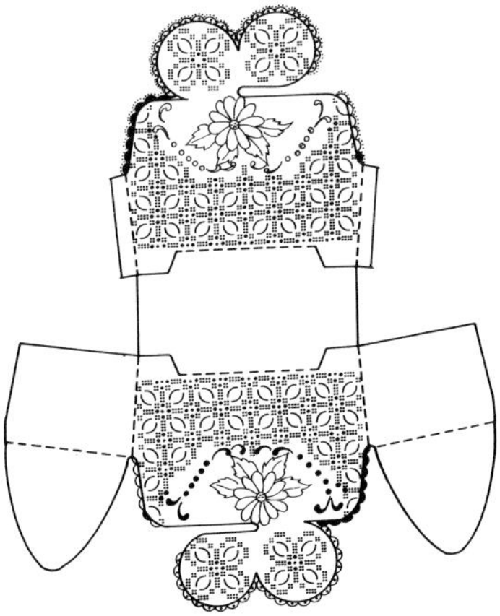

piece of work no. 6

BOX WITH BOW

Tracing
With a white pencil: the contours and folding lines; Tinta white: the scalloped lines.

Perforating
As in perforation patterns.

Embossing
The decorations marked in black; the scalloped lines, the folding lines.

Cutting
Cut the 4-hole perforations into cross-shaped holes and slits.

Perforating and cutting out
Cut out the lay-out; perforate and cut out as indicated by the dotted lines.

Folding
Fold the box (no glueing required).

Finishing off
Attach the side flaps to each other with a bright coloured ribbon of 4 mm width: slip it through the perforations and finish in a bow.

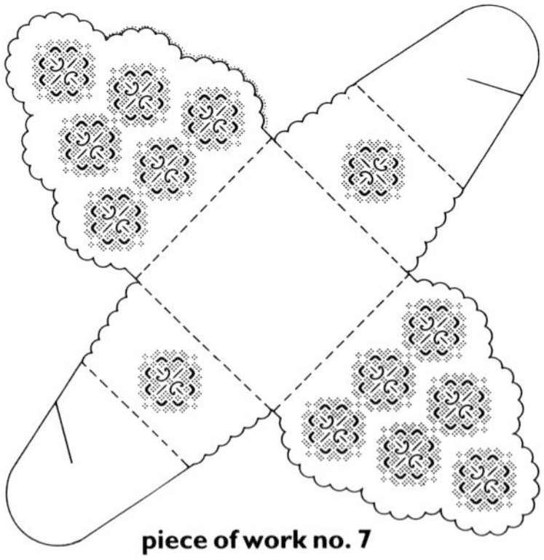

piece of work no. 7

WATER LILY

General
The water lily has been attached to the leaves with a copper split pin (used to close sample envelopes). You could also glue the parts together. The lily can be opened and closed.

Tracing
Tinta white: the contours and folding lines.

Dorsing
Dorso pink: the surfaces 1.
Dorso turquoise: the surfaces 2 and the leaves.

Perforating
As in perforation patterns.

Embossing
The crosses marked in black; the decorative lines around the perforations, the dots, the veins of the leaves and the folding lines. N.B.: emboss on the front side: the hexagon x-x-x-x-x-x- and the lines 2.

Cutting
Cut the 4-hole perforations into cross-shaped holes and slits.

Perforating and cutting out
Perforate and cut out the water lily, the leaves and the round hole in the centre of the water lily.

Folding
Fold upwards on the lines A-C, B-D, D-F, E-A, C-E, F-B and flatten the folds (the six sides of the hexagon). Fold the half circle lines backwards on the lines A-B, B-C, C-D, D-E, E-F, and F-A. Rub over the folding lines 2 with your thumb and forefinger. Finally, from the outside, fold the lines A-X, B-X etc.

Finishing off
leaves Attach the water lily to the leaves with a split pin through holes 1 and 2.

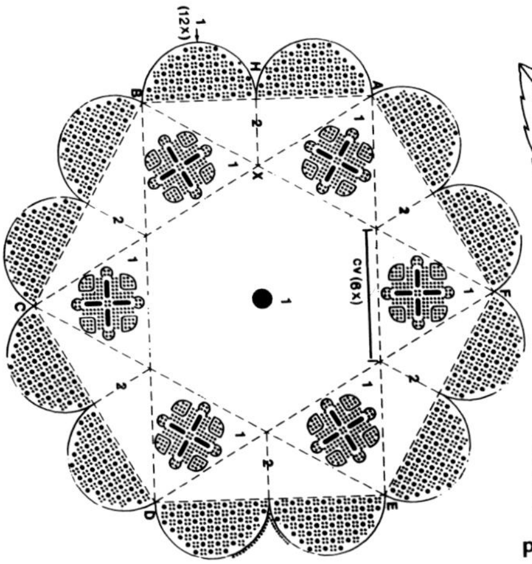

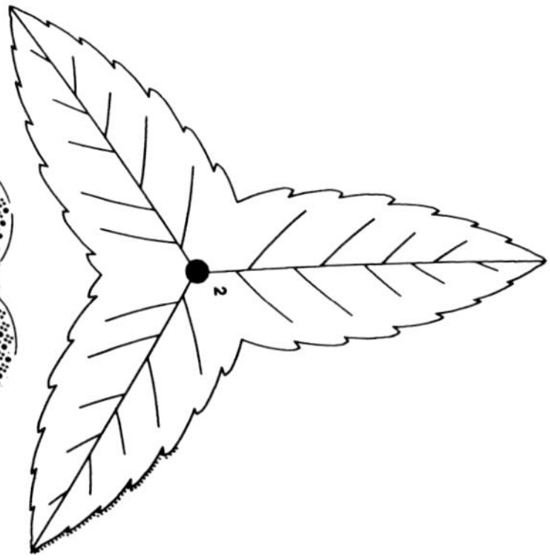

piece of work no. 8

BASKET

General

two parts

This pattern has two parts: the basket and the handle. Two ribbons (pink and purple) of 3 mm. width have been laced through the handle.

Tracing

With a white pencil: the contours and folding lines.

Dorsing

Dorso purple: the surfaces 1.
Dorso pink: the surfaces 2.

Perforating

As in perforation patterns.

Embossing

The dots and decorations as indicated in the perforation patterns; the scalloped edge of the basket.

small ball embossing tool

Use the small ball embossing tool to emboss the folding lines as indicated.

stylus

Use the stylus to emboss the hearts (the parts indicated in black).

Cutting

Cut the 4-hole perforations into cross-shaped holes and slits. The handle: cut the connections between the perforations along the contours of the handle and take off superfluous paper.

Folding

Fold the basket in its hexagonal shape: fold the surfaces nos. 2 upwards and the surfaces nos. I downwards (see picture). Fold back the perforations with the scalloped edges of the surfaces 2 with the exception of the two that will be used to attach the handle to.

Finishing off

ribbon

Lace a pink and a purple ribbon of 3 mm width through the perforations (alternate them). Attach the handle to the outside of the basked on the spot 'H' with needle and thread. Cover the attachment with a small bow.

piece of work no. 9

HEXAGONAL BOX

Tracing
With a white pencil: all contours and folding lines; Tinta white: the scalloped lines.

Dorsing
Dorso blue: the surfaces 1.

Perforating
As in perforation patterns.

Embossing
The decorations marked in black, the dots in the perforation patterns, the scalloped lines, the folding lines.

Cutting
Cut the 4-hole perforations into cross-shaped holes and slits. Cut the scalloped lines 'G' with the Pergamano scissors, they have to have a smooth edge.

Perforating and cutting out
Cut out the lay-out; perforate and cut out as indicated by the dotted lines. Cut out the parts 'X'.

Folding and glueing
folding direction

Fold the box and glue the seven glueing strips. Fold the rest of the lines of the top lid and mind the folding direction.

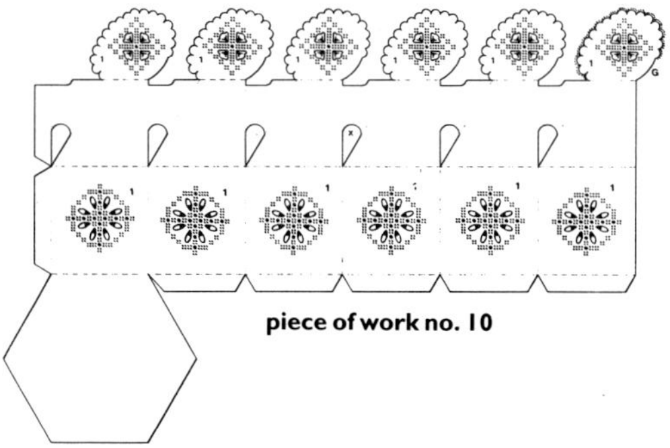

piece of work no. 10

RECTANGULAR BOX

(look at the step by step pictures)

Tracing
With a white pencil: all contours and folding lines; Tinta white: the flowers, the scalloped lines; Tinta sepia: the leaves, the stalks.

Dorsing
Dorso purple: the surfaces 1.

Painting
Pintura white + fuchsia: the petals; Pintura green + yellow + brown: the leaves; Pintura yellow + brown: the flower hearts.

Perforating
As in perforation patterns.

Embossing
The decorations marked in black, the flowers, the folding lines, the dots.

Cutting
Cut the 4-hole perforations into cross-shaped holes and slits.

Perforating and cutting out
Cut out the lay-out; perforate and cut out as indicated by the dotted lines like the parts 'E'.

Folding and glueing
Fold the box as follows: fold the long folding lines x-x and the glueing strips three times; fold the oblique lines (marked 'cv'); fold the lines A-B (2x) and C-D (2x).
Fold all lines in the proper direction.
Glue the 3 glueing strips. Turn both ends of the box a quarter turn, and move them a bit towards the inside at the same time.

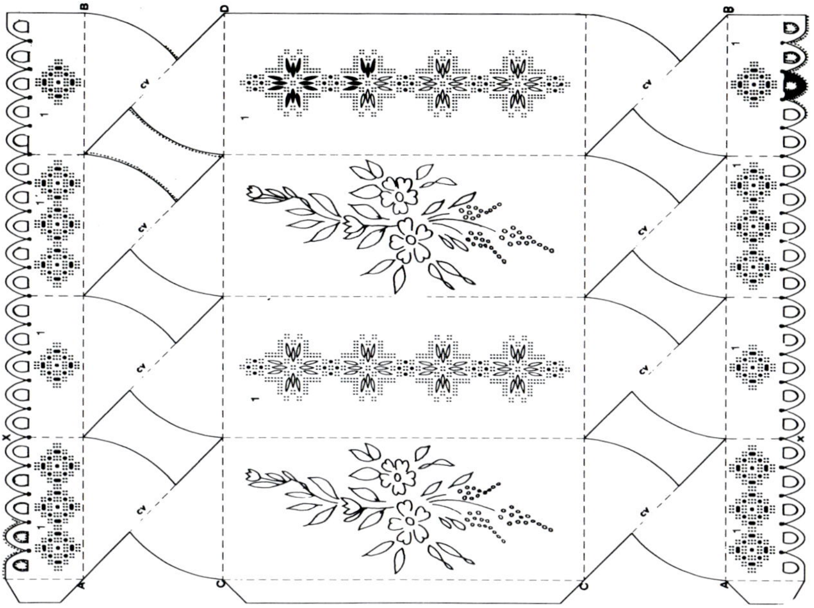

piece of work no. 11

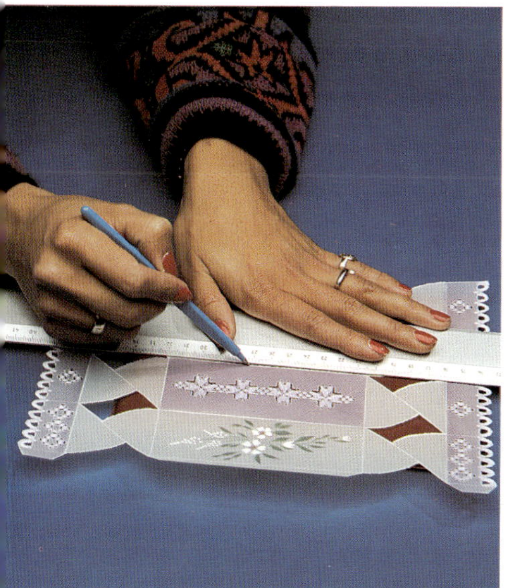

LITTLE HOUSE

General

red ribbon

A red ribbon of 5 mm width is laced through the roof. Total length of the ribbon: 110 cm.

Tracing

With a white pencil: the contours and folding lines; Tinta white: the windows, doors and flowerpots.

Painting

Pintura green: the windows, doors and leaves (very fine); Pintura red: the flowerpots; Pintura fuchsia: the flowers.

Perforating

As in perforation patterns.

Embossing

The decorations marked in black; the curtains, the scalloped lines and the folding lines.

Cutting

Cut the 4-hole perforations into cross-shaped holes and slits.

Perforating and cutting out

Cut out all the contours of the lay-out, cut in the incision (for the insert) at the back of the roof.

Lacing the ribbon

Lace the ribbon through the perforations of the roof and cut it to measure at the sides.

Folding and glueing

overlap of the roof

Fold the house, the front side the house has an overlapping roof. Glue the vertical glueing strips. Fold the bottom as indicated by the numbers. The plain part of the roof is folded downwards at the back of the house. Insert the folded flap into the incision in the roof.

ANGEL

General

extra materials

To make the angel, the following extra materials are required: 1 cotton ball with a diameter of 38 mm., 1 cocktail stick, a bit of angel hair (= material for dolls), glitter powder. The angel consists of 5 parts: the dress, 2 sleeves, a collar and the wings.

Tracing

Tinta blue: the scalloped lines, the flowers; Tinta gold: the contours of the wings, a line outside the blue scalloped lines, the decorative lines on the sleeves.

Dorsing

Dorso blue: the whole sheet of parchment paper, size A4.

Perforating

As in perforation patterns.

Embossing

The decorations marked in black and the scalloped lines.

Cutting

Cut the 4-hole perforations into cross-shaped holes and slits.

Perforating and cutting out

Cut along the straight lines, perforate and cut out as indicated by the dotted lines.

Folding and glueing

Fold the dress and sleeves into cones and glue the glueing strips.

Making the wings

Pergakit glitter powder

Put some Pergakit on the wings and rub it out over the total surface of the wings. Immediately sprinkle some glitter powder onto the wings. Let superfluous glitter powder fall off onto a sheet of paper so you can use it again.

Making the head

a fine brush

Paint the face with a fine brush, making very fine and delicate lines. Pintura black: the contours of the eyes, mouth and nose; Pintura red: the mouth. Paint the eyes blue, with a black pupil. Dorso pink: blushes on the cheeks.

Finishing off

Pergakit

Glue the sleeves against the sides of the dress with Pergakit; be careful: the perforations in the dress should be exactly in the middle, and the glueing strip of the sleeves should be glued against the dress. Glue a cocktail stick into the top of the dress – let it stick out 15 mm. Attach the collar with a bit of Pergakit. Attach the hair to the head with a bit of glue. Make a small hole in the head. Glue the head onto the cocktail stick.

drying

Attach the wings to the back of the dress with a lot of Pergakit; add extra Pergakit between the vertical wings and the cone-shaped dress to fill up the distance between the two. To dry, lay the angel on a table, wings down.

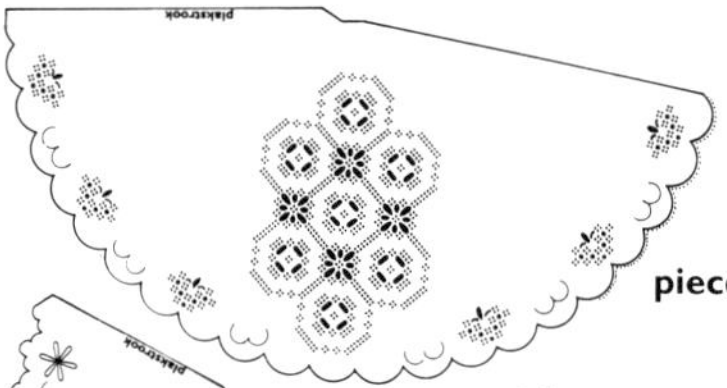

piece of work no.13-sleeve

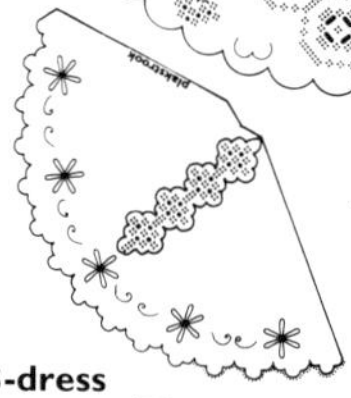

piece of work no.13-dress

piece of work no.13-collar

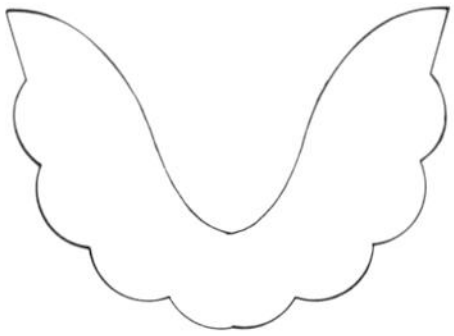

piece of work no.13-wing

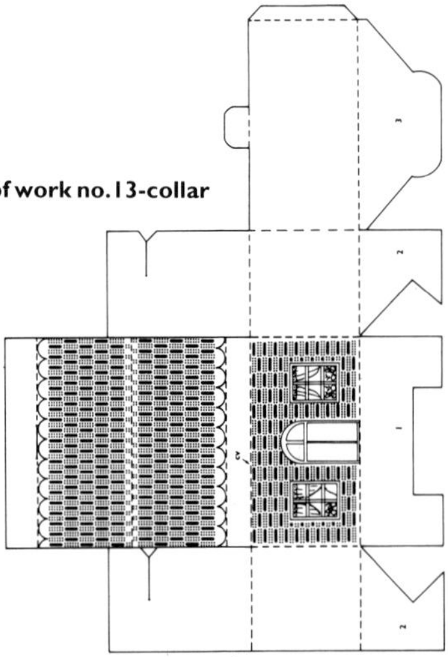

piece of work no. 14

CRADLE

Tracing
With a white pencil: the contours and folding lines; Tinta white: the scalloped lines.

Dorsing
Dorso pink: the whole lay-out, except for the glueing strips.

Perforating
As in perforation patterns.

Embossing
The scalloped lines, the dots and vertical hatching in the decorations.

Cutting
crosses Cut the 4-hole perforations into cross-shaped holes.

Perforating and cutting out
Cut out the lay-out; perforate and cut out as indicated by the dotted lines. Cut out the contours of the legs.

Folding and glueing
lay-out Fold the lay-out into a cradle and glue the glueing strip. Fold the bottom of the cradle: first 1, then 2, 3 and 4.

Finishing off
ribbon Lace a pink ribbon of 2 mm width through the perforations and finish it off with glued-on bows (see picture). Bring the three top parts of the cradle together by lacing a ribbon through the 3 holes and finish it off with a bow.

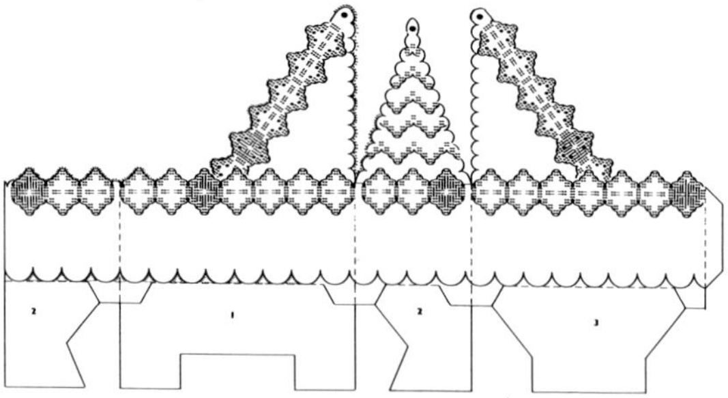

piece of work no. 12

MOBILE

General

5 items florist's wire nylon thread

The mobile consists of 5 pieces of work (5 items). These items are attached with nylon thread to the 2 horizontal bars of florist's wire.
In the hobby shops you can buy special wire for mobiles. Length required: 20 cms each.

Extra materials required

Two bars of wire for mobiles or florist's wire and 2 meters of thin nylon thread.

Tracing

With a white pencil: the contours and folding lines of all the pieces of work; Tinta white: the flowers and scalloped lines.
Trace all the other patterns in the colours as indicated: T. wi = Tinta white, T. bl = Tinta blue, T. ro = Tinta red, T. ge = Tinta yellow.
N.B.: trace part no. 2 twice (= front and back side of the star).

Dorsing

Dorse as indicated in the pattern: D. bl = Dorso blue, D. ge = Dorso yellow, D. ro = Dorso red, D. gr = Dorso green.

Perforating

As in perforation patterns.

Embossing

The decorations marked in black and the scalloped lines.

Cutting

Cut the 4-hole perforations into cross-shaped holes and slits.

Perforating and cutting out

Cut out the lay-outs; perforate and cut out as indicated by the dotted lines.

Folding and glueing

Fold the pieces of work into the shapes you see in the pictures. Glue the glueing strips. Mount the two parts of the star like a box and lid.

Finishing off

mounting Mount the pieces of work as follows: With a nylon thread you hang piece of work no. 1 at one end of the top bar and the second bar at the other end of the top bar, in the middle you hang piece of work no. 2. At either end of the second bar you hang piece of work no. 3 and no. 4, and in the middle: no. 5. Vary the length of the nylon threads to create a playful effect.

balance Attach a thread in the middle of the top bar and shift till the two bars are in balance (horizontal). Fix the attachment points with a bit of glue.

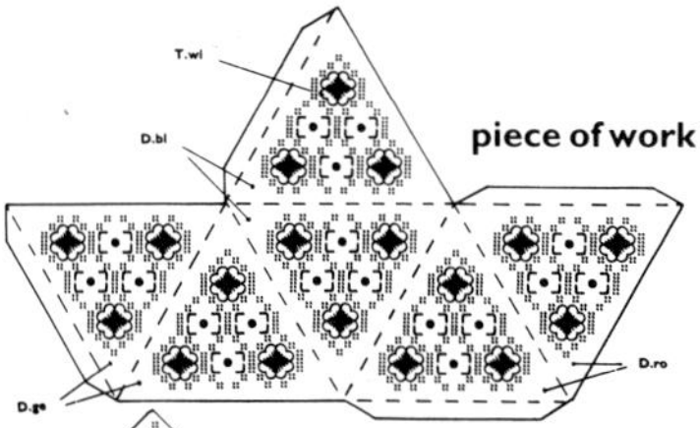

piece of work no. 15 – item 3

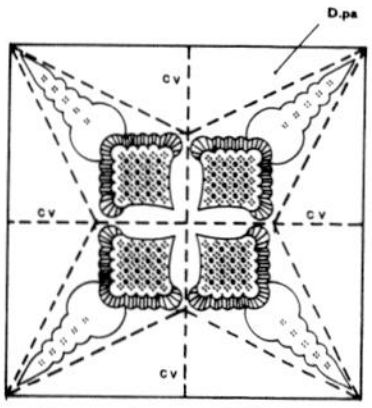

piece of work no. 15 – item 2

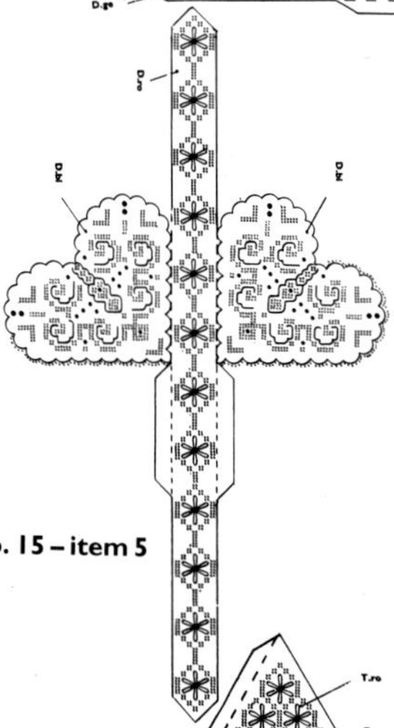

piece of work no. 15 – item 5

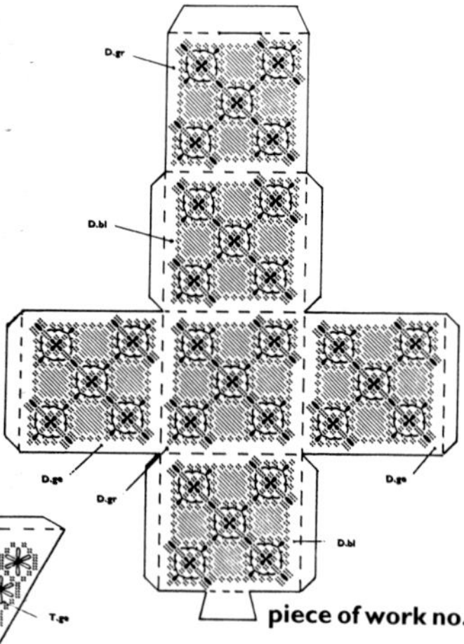

piece of work no. 15 – item

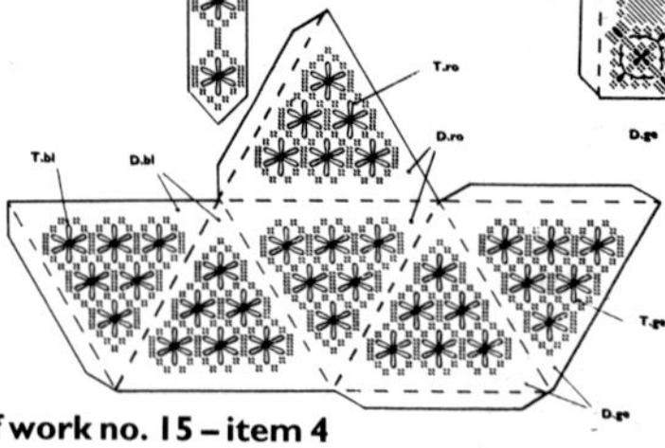

piece of work no. 15 – item 4